THE **KID** FROM CALIFORNIA

DELVIN CHATTERSON

THE KID FROM CALIFORNIA

DELVIN CHATTERSON

THE KID FROM CALIFORNIA

SHORT STORIES - VOLUME I
DELVIN CHATTERSON

ISBN: 978-1-0689279-3-5 Print paperback
ISBN: 978-1-0689279-4-2 E-Book

Published by:
Uncle Ralph's Publishing Empire
(Division of 146152 Canada Inc.)

TABLE OF CONTENTS

INTRODUCTION

The Kid from California Short Story Series was inspired by my reading of the early pulp fiction detective novels of Raymond Chandler, Dashiell Hammett, and Robert B. Parker, followed by David Baldacci's Archer Series which convincingly demonstrates that those stories and their stereotypical characters can be updated to appeal to modern readers.

The series is also based on my personal knowledge of Southern California – Palm Springs, in particular – and the history of the Mob in Las Vegas, Nevada. The main character, Patrick Malloy, is a young man from San Diego trying to get ahead in the 1960s while working as an enforcer for the gangsters and occasionally as a bodyguard for Frank Sinatra. Those themes offer lots of possibilities for dark and dangerous stories mixed with a young man's angst, moral dilemmas, and a few romantic episodes.

In these three stories, Patrick is trying to stay true to himself and his own moral code while working for the Mafia owner of a Las Vegas casino. He's continually challenged to avoid becoming a murderous gangster without becoming a victim himself.

Del Chatterson
December 2024

MY WAY

MY WAY

I was sitting alone in a red leather booth along the back wall facing the front door like a gunfighter in a Western movie waiting for the bad guys. Only I was not in a dusty saloon with a bunch of cowboys, I was in a posh restaurant called The Mexicali Mesa Roadhouse a few miles from Palm Springs, California, sitting with one of those movie stars and the most famous celebrity in town, Mr. Frank Sinatra. He was seated in a booth to my left a few yards away.

But I was waiting for the bad guys to show up. One in particular, named Saul Gohlen, had been invited to meet me here. I put down the menu and reached for my beer to take a sip and watch a black Desoto with its distinctive slanted tailfins and twin headlights pull into the parking lot out front and park next to my '59 Caddy. It was starting to look like a gangster parking lot with the big black sedans lined up outside.

Not a problem. Maybe it keeps out the riff raff who can't afford this place and keeps the fans away from Mr.

Sinatra so I don't have to step in and ask them to back away. It's usually a bigger problem in Vegas where the fans come from far away and are determined to see him up close and personal. He's still the biggest draw in Vegas and the casino owners want to take good care of him. That's why my boss at the Golden Goose Casino, Mr. Bruno Giovanni, calls on me occasionally to make sure he gets home safely to Palm Springs away from the crowds. "Take him home and tuck him in at night," he tells me. I usually stay a few days and then drive back to Vegas, sometimes with Mr. Sinatra, sometimes alone. It's good to have the Caddy for the long drive. It was a nice bonus for my boss to give me his car after he traded up to a new one.

I saw Saul Gohlen get out of the back seat of the Desoto and his driver led him to the front door of the restaurant. I knew them both. The driver, Donnie Bronson, is another kid from small town California like me, trying to work his way up the food chain of gangsters in Vegas as a driver, tough guy, enforcer, bodyguard, whatever they offered us. We both have the necessary credentials – big and strong, and hungry for the money. Donnie had been a high school football player too, I think. He's built big like a lineman and not too bright. I'm lighter, faster and smarter, and played as a running back in high school. I wouldn't want to take him on in a fist fight. I could probably wrestle him to the ground, but not hold him down. It'd take two or three slugs from a big gun to take him down. My hand went to the holster under my arm and I patted the .38 through my suit jacket.

I noticed Donnie and Gohlen were checking the perimeter for any trouble as they crossed the parking lot. They did the same as they came in the door to the restaurant. Good to see they were a little nervous. Gohlen lifted his eyebrows as he recognized Sinatra in the booth, then squinted trying to recognize the dark-haired young man he was sitting with. Donnie scanned the room and saw I was alone in a booth at the back. He nodded at Gohlen and went back out to slouch on the front fender of the Desoto and light a cigarette.

Gohlen arrived at my booth and sat at the end where he could take a better look at Sinatra and his dinner partner. "Hello Patrick," he said. "I got the message you wanted to meet me here. You gonna introduce me to Sinatra?"

"Nope. They pay me to keep people away from him."

He smirked, then squinted again at Sinatra's booth. "Is that Paul Anka he's with?"

"Yeah. They're taking a break from the shows up in Vegas and working on some new songs, I think."

He turned to face me and sat back, relaxing comfortably into the booth.

"OK, so why'd you want to see me, Patrick?"

I pushed the menu toward him. "You want dinner? I'm buying."

"No thanks. I presume I'm not here for dinner, anyway. You got something else for me?"

"How about a beer before I start on what I got for you?" I didn't wait for an answer. I took a moment to catch the waiter's eye and signal for another beer, same as mine. I wanted to let Gohlen sweat a little. We waited for the beer to arrive and the waiter to get out of earshot again. Gohlen patiently held the poker face and didn't look worried.

"OK, here's the deal," I said. "I've been sent by Mr. Giovanni to have a little chat with you." It was not entirely true, but only a small lie.

"You heard from his brother already and you know they're not happy about you stepping on their toes in Vegas. They told you to back off and stay away, but you didn't do that. You keep on coming into their territory."

Gohlen's narrow face hardened and he took a deep breath. To calm himself or to put up a brave front? I wasn't sure until he spoke.

"Giovanni doesn't scare me," he said.

His denial meant the opposite. He was worried. Maybe he'd poked the wrong bear one too many times. He continued.

"I told them we should work together." He was starting to whine. "I can help them make more money. Why can't we do that?"

"But Saul, they don't need your help to make more money. You have to wait to be invited, if you want to work with Giovani."

His eyes dropped to the table and he seemed to shrink into his suit jacket.

"You made a big mistake," I said, "sending your guys into the casino trying to poach customers and dealers for your own poker rooms. They kill people for that kinda stuff in Vegas. You were warned to back off and instead your guys show up again on Giovanni's turf."

I let that sink in.

Now he was sweating. He pulled his necktie away from his throat and swallowed.

I said, "So you have one last chance to fix this, Saul. No more talk. You do or you die." He was looking more nervous and peered at me, listening closely.

I said, "You need to prove you know how to play by the rules, if you're gonna work with these guys."

He looked up and his face was hopeful. "Yeah, what? Sure. What can I do to prove myself."

I gave him a grim look. "You know these guys believe it's kill or be killed, right? So that's the deal. You have to kill a guy for them or be killed yourself."

His face fell. He leaned toward me and said in a harsh whisper, "I'm not a killer! I won't do that." He was shaking his head at the proposition.

"There must be another way," he said.

"Nope. No other way. And it has to be done tonight."

I let him chew on it quietly a moment longer.

He looked around anxiously and lifted his head to see if Donnie was nearby. He was back in the driver's seat of the Desoto with the window open and his arm resting on the side, blowing smoke out of the car.

Gohlen's eyes came back to me and I said to him, "What about your guy Donnie out there, is he up to it?"

Suddenly, he looked hopeful again. "Yeah. Yeah, he'd do it. He wants to prove he's a killer. I'll get him to do it. That's a good idea. We can do that."

I waited a moment to let him think about what he had just agreed to do for us. "OK, good," I said.

Gohlen sucked in a long breath and asked, "So what do you need from us?"

I slid the menu aside and leaned in, speaking softly, slowly and clearly.

"Here's the plan. Meet me tonight at 11:30 sharp. I'll be at a picnic area in the desert, on the road to Joshua Tree Park. Go twenty-seven miles east of town on Highway 10, then north towards the park about three miles and make a right off the road at the sign for the picnic area. It's about a quarter mile in along a dry creek bed. Bring Donnie and be sure he's armed. You have a gun too, Saul?"

"Yeah, I'll bring one, but Donnie does the killing, right?"

"That's the plan" I said and watched him take a hard swallow to digest the message. He hadn't touched his beer yet.

"You got it, Saul?"

"Yeah, yeah, I got it." He mumbled to himself, "… twenty-seven miles east, north three miles, turn right, … picnic area at 11:30 sharp."

"Good," I said. "Now I'm gonna have my dinner. See you later."

I lifted the menu and nodded to Gohlen as he got up and left. His glass of beer was still on the table.

* * *

In the Caddy on the way back to Mr. Sinatra's house, we drove back from the restaurant through La Quinta toward Palm Springs and his quiet neighbourhood under the palm trees to the northwest along Highway 111 though the centre of Palm Desert past the brightly lit strip malls, motels, restaurants and night clubs. It wasn't the bright lights of Vegas, but Palm Springs was a popular oasis in the desert just about two-and-a-half hours away for anyone escaping the frantic life of Los Angeles and Hollywood. Not many could afford a second luxury home here like the Hollywood stars, but there were good choices for everyone visiting – from the low-priced motel hangouts and diners to the exclusive resorts, restaurants, and golf clubs for the rich and famous.

Mr. Sinatra sat back in the seat out of sight and watched the scenery go by. We'd spent a lot of time in the car together and had come to know each other pretty well. He was a gentleman – not a snob who wouldn't give any notice to a kid from Southern California trying to make his way among the big shots and gangsters in Las Vegas. On the longer trips, about four-and-a-half hours from Las Vegas to either of his homes in Beverley Hills or Palm Springs, sometimes he dozed or wrote replies to his fan mail or worked on the other paperwork he pulled out of his briefcase. Sometimes we chatted.

He was well-known as a suave, sophisticated, debonair ladies' man – not like me, rough around the edges, though I was doing all right with the gorgeous dames in Las Vegas, too. They think I'm ruggedly handsome, apparently. But old blue eyes, he makes their hearts skip a beat. He's had that effect on the ladies for a long time. I'm just taking care of business and trying not to get too distracted by all the opportunities to go astray.

I asked him, "How did your dinner meeting go tonight with Mr. Anka? You looked pretty busy there."

"It was good, Patrick, the dinner and the meeting," he said.

He caught my eye in the rear-view mirror. "He's a talented kid, that charming young Canadian – full of energy, kinda like me when I was that age. And he's a great songwriter, too." His velvety voice filled the car and it was a pleasure to listen to him even if he wasn't singing. My own voice always sounded pretty thin and not very musical at all, when I replied.

He continued. "Anka's working on a new song for me. He thinks it'll be my signature song, if we get it right. It's about no regrets, how I always did it my way. It could be a hit all right. We need to put up something good against Elvis and the Beatles. They're getting all the attention these days, on the radio and the Billboard charts."

He nodded to himself and looked out the window again as we pulled up to a traffic light. "But I'm not sure I like it. It seems kind of boastful, and I don't like that."

"Oh no, Mr. Sinatra," I said, "you don't have to worry about that. You're not singing about yourself, you're singin' for the rest of us who ain't got the words like you and Mr. Anka." I could see him smiling in the rear-view mirror and he looked back at me with a tilt of his head as he thought about it.

I told him, "It's like them books I been reading about Mike Hammer and them other tough guys, they're doin' it their way too. That's what we all want."

We drove on in silence for a bit after that. Then he said, "I see you had a meeting tonight at Mexicali Mesa too, Patrick. Are you working two jobs at the same time now?"

"Well, kinda," I said. "Two jobs for the same boss, anyway. You're always my first priority of course, Mr.

Sinatra, but while I was having dinner there, I had another meeting for Mr. Giovanni."

I glanced at him in the mirror. "I'm going to have to go out later tonight to work on another job, but I'll get you settled at home first and then set the alarm system for when I'm out. I hope that's alright, sir."

"No problem," he said. "But don't take on too much for Giovanni, Patrick. He's willing to use you up and throw you away, anytime. Remember what your mother told you, 'You can't burn the candle at both ends without getting your fingers burnt.' You've got to take care of yourself."

"Yes, sir. I'm trying to do that."

Tonight would be a test of how far I was willing to go for Mr. Bruno Giovanni and still take care of myself.

* * *

A few hours later, I find myself sitting in the dark in the desert on a rough, grey weathered wooden picnic table. There are two more picnic tables behind me on a flat strip of hard dusty ground above a dry creek bed that hasn't seen a flash flood all year. Maybe in many years. On the hillside to the north a few scrawny palm trees are silhouetted against the dark sky and I know the twisted shapes of Joshua trees and prickly flowering cactus are hidden in the shadows. No place for a hike in the dark. There's a faint scent of sage in the air that helps clear my mind.

I need to focus on the plan. I hope it's a good plan, but I've gotta be ready for surprises. I know people don't aways do what they say they'll do. I don't see any car lights out on the paved road that runs north past the picnic site. I turned in here about half an hour ago and parked the Caddy on the side of the small parking lot that's outlined by rows of round boulders from the creek bed. I'm facing the exit, ready to leave in a hurry if I have to.

But I really don't want to be here at all. I know I'm still working my way up the ladder inside Giovanni's organisation and he already trusts me enough to look after Mr. Sinatra, but tonight will be my first killing for him. And he wants me to do two of them if necessary.

Killing changes everything. There's no going back from that, only onward and upward in the world of crime, hopefully to better things. Do I really need better than I have it now? What about the delightful Denise I'm so sweet on? She seems sweet on me too and likes it when I'm hanging around with Mr. Sinatra and the other celebrities in Vegas. I don't think she'll ever want to know about what I'm up to tonight. Like I said to Gohlen, it's kill or be killed. But the other side of the coin is if you're willing to kill somebody, you better be ready to get killed yourself. The people coming after you next know you won't be stopped by anything else.

I see the twin-beam headlights of the Desoto turn off the paved road and wind its way toward me. As it approaches, the lights find me seated on the picnic bench and I point toward a space on the other side of the lot so they can pull in with the headlights pointing up the gulch below the picnic tables and along the dry creek bed. I might need lights in that direction later. The lights go off and the cooling engine clicks in the cool, quiet darkness of the desert as Donnie and Gohlen get out and close the doors quietly.

They look around and get used to the dark. I get up and walk to meet them beside my car. Gohlen looks agitated.

He says, "OK, we're here, right on time. Now what?"

"Let me see your weapons," I say. "Then I'll explain what happens next." I hold my .38 revolver out so they can see it's loaded and point it down.

Gohlen looks around us and back down the road away from the picnic area.

"Where's the guy?" he says.

"Oh, he's here," I tell him.

He looks at the big, closed trunk of my Caddy. I know there's nobody in the trunk, just a pick and shovel I'd grabbed from Mr. Sinatra's garden shed before leaving his house. Gohlen shows me his small .22 calibre pistol, then quickly slips it back in his coat pocket before I can ask him to use it.

I look at Donnie who's holding out a more serious-looking Colt .45 in the palm of his meaty hand. I wonder if I'm about to make the biggest mistake of my life or if I might just have a plan that gets me out of here alive.

I look Donnie in the eye. "Are you loaded and ready to go?"

He nods, and I say, "OK, let's do it."

Donnie grips the gun in his fist and turns to point it at Gohlen's chest just inches away. "Sorry, Mr. G," he says. "I got a better offer."

Gohlen panics and reaches for the gun in his pocket, but there's a flash of fire from the muzzle of Donnie's gun and three loud shots plow into Gohlen's chest knocking him backwards. A fourth shot rips into his belly as he falls to the ground and lies sprawled flat on his back with his eyes and mouth wide open. Blood gurgles in his throat. The loud gunshots fade into the wide-open spaces of the desert without any echo bouncing back. Donnie takes two steps forward and places the muzzle above Gohlen's left eye and blows his brains into the dirt.

He turns toward me with a look of proud satisfaction, holding the gun down by his side as smoke curls from the barrel and around his thigh. The scent of sage is replaced by the corrosive smell of gunpowder. I feel like I've released a madman from Hell.

I raise my gun and make a decision. This is where I'm supposed to kill Donnie and place my gun in Gohlen's hand to make it look like a shoot-out that killed them both. I put the gun back in the shoulder holster under my arm.

"OK, Donnie, you're hired."

I pull out a roll of thousand-dollar bills from my pants pocket. I peel off five thousand and hand it to him. Giovanni had paid me ten thousand in cash and I figure Donnie earned half.

I look at him holding five thousand in one hand and his gun in the other. He's staring at the wad of cash I'm stuffing back in my pocket.

Am I nuts? Is this how I want this to end? Here and now?

I turn my back on him and start toward the trunk of my car.

"OK, let's clean this up and get outa here," I say over my shoulder. "You need to get back to town and work on your alibi. Hang out in a bar tonight, be conspicuous. Then check-out tomorrow, after you discover Gohlen is missing. Say nothing and go home. Look me up in Vegas in a couple of weeks and I'll find more work for you."

I open the trunk and reach in for the pick and shovel.

Donnie comes up beside me. He's smiling and patting his pocket with the five grand in it. "Anything you need that pays this good, I'm ready for it," he says.

I hand him the pick and keep the shovel. "Let's start with a shallow grave for your recently deceased boss."

I gesture past the picnic tables along the ridge above the gulch where the Desoto is pointing, but I decide to leave the headlights off since we're less noticeable from the road in the dark.

Donnie drops his .45 into the side pocket of his suit jacket then slings the jacket over his shoulder and heads up the gulch, carrying the pick like a miner heading into the hills.

I lean the shovel against the open trunk and take out a brown canvas tarp and walk back to the body of Saul Gohlen. Blood is soaking into the dirt all around him and I spread out the tarp to cover the whole deadly mess. We can haul it all away in the tarp and throw it in the shallow grave on the hillside when we're ready.

I go back past my car to pick up the shovel and close the trunk before heading after Donnie. I can hear the rhythmic thump of the pick as he plunges it into the hardpan in the gulch. I'm remembering Mr. Sinatra's smile in the mirror earlier this evening.

Yeah, the job's done, and I did it my way. I ain't singin' it though.

* * *

LOOKING
FOR WORK
WELCOME
TO Fabulous
LAS VEGAS
NEVADA

LOOKING FOR WORK

It took Donnie Bronson a while to find me in Vegas after the killing of his boss, Saul Goshen. I should've known he'd be looking for me, since he was now out of work and I'd promised to help him out. I worked in security for Mr. Bruno Giovanni at the Golden Goose Casino and that's where he found me.

Unfortunately, when he found me, I was rushing through the casino to the dining room to see Denise Callahan who had called and wanted to see me right away. So I put Donnie off until the next day and told him to meet me in the lounge on the main floor.

When I arrived in the dining room and saw Denise working the tables, it gave me a thrill as usual at the sight of her, even though she was primly dressed for work in a long black skirt and plain white blouse. It hit me harder when she looked over, flicked the blonde curls back from her face, and gave me a wide smile before tilting her head toward the door to the kitchen. I walked over there and waited for her.

A minute later, she came back from taking the guests' orders into the kitchen and reached out to gently squeeze my hand – no kissing in the dining room. But the squeeze was enough to get me in the mood to hold her tight and satisfy the urge for more. She leaned close, as I held myself in check, and said, "Patrick, don't look now, but over there sitting at the table by the middle column, there's three guys I thought you should know about."

I kept my attention on her and glanced quickly to the table and the three guys she was talking about. "Yeah. What about 'em?"

"I think they're talking about your boss."

That was something I should know about. I knew they didn't work for Giovanni at the Casino, and they didn't look like cops. "What did you hear them saying?"

"I just heard Mr. Giovanni's name and the older one said something about 'they'd have to take care of it.' Then they shut up when they realized I was near their table."

"Thanks Denise, you're right to call me. I don't like the sound of it. They look like tough guys from somewhere. I'll have to find out more what they're up to. Don't you worry about it."

She nodded, turned away and went back to work. I watched her swaying backside go between the tables and disappear through the kitchen door again, then I went in the opposite direction and avoided letting the three guys see my face in case they had noticed me with Denise. I went out the side door and after a few moments in the back hallway, I came back around to the dining room entrance and chatted to the maître d' while giving them another sideways look. All three were mean-looking tough guys in dark suits, but not our tough guys. The older one short and fat, one tall and skinny, one big all over. The big guy was shaved bald, skinny had long greasy hair swept back behind his ears, and Fatso looked like the boss – older, better suit – and he did most of the talking while the other two listened and nodded at whatever he was saying. I left and went to sit in the front lobby where I could wait and watch for them to come out of the dining room.

When they did, they walked straight toward the front doors, then Fatso veered off across the casino floor while the two others headed for the parking lot in front. Fatso went over to the semicircle of blackjack tables and titled his head at the pit boss to come out from his spot behind the dealers and meet him off to the side. He came around with a friendly smile and they shook hands and joked a bit, then chatted a while, looking more serious. After another hard handshake, Fatso left to join his buddies in the Oldsmobile sedan that had pulled up to the front entrance. Baldy was driving and Skinny sat in the back so Fatso could have the front passenger seat. I watched them leave, turn left onto the Strip and head north toward

Caesar's Palace and the Flamingo, then the car slipped out of site in the traffic and disappeared from view.

I went back into the casino and walked across to speak to the pit boss standing behind the blackjack dealers. An old-timer, grey hair, and tired squinting eyes, the years he'd spent in casinos showed in his dark lined face. His name was Samuel Camino, but we called him Sammy the Shark. He used to be a card shark. Now he was paid to keep an eye out for the troublemakers trying to beat the odds at the Golden Goose.

As I approached him, he said, "Hi Patrick, keeping us safe these days?"

"Doin' my best," I said. "But I have a question for you, Sammy, what's up with the fat guy you were talking to here, a few minutes ago."

"Oh, him? He's an old friend from when I worked at the Stardust. The name's Benny Fontaine. He looks after security for Max Palermo now, over at the Fortune Palace. He's not as fat as he looks, by the way. Hard as nails. Strong like a bull. Big meaty hands, he nearly crushes my damn fingers every time we shake hands, the sonofabitch." He grinned and tilted his head with a shrug.

"I see. What did he have to say that kept you chatting for a bit?"

"Actually, he had a message for the boss. Maybe you can deliver it for me, Patrick. It's more your department than mine. You're Bruno's tough guy, I'm just a pit boss on the floor."

Now he had my attention. "OK, sure. What was the message?"

"The message for Bruno was that Palermo wants to arrange a meeting. So the two of them can decide what they want to do – make peace or declare war."

"Hmmm, … interesting. I'll speak to Mr. Giovanni and give him the message. I'm not sure what he'll think of it, they're supposed to have a peace deal already. You think Palermo is delivering a warning the peace is over?"

"He didn't say it was a warning, but you may be right. Sounds like Palermo is giving

Bruno a last chance before he declares war. A meeting might be a good idea to prevent it."

"Fatso's name is Benny Fontaine, you said?" Sammy nodded.

* * *

When Donnie found me again the next day, he insisted on pulling me aside to sit at a corner table in the lounge away from the chatter of excited gamblers and the jangling of change at the slot machines. Even at three in the afternoon the casino was too noisy a spot for a quiet chat.

"You're hard to track down, Patrick," he said. "I'm looking for that job you promised. The cash you paid me in Palm Springs is running out." He broke into a wide grin, then leaned forward to whisper, "Anybody else I can whack for you?"

I backed away from him. *What the hell?*

"I don't know what you're talking about Donnie." I paused and gave him a scowl to shut him up. "I don't have any work for you here. There's nothing I can do for you right now. Maybe come back another time."

He was shocked and sat back looking confused. "What do you mean? Back in the dark in the desert – you gotta remember."

He frowned at me. Then he realized what he was saying.

He gave me an awkward shrug. "Yeah, you're right. I don't know what I'm talking about." He thought about it for a moment. "OK, let me put it this way, Patrick. Remember when we met at the diner in Palm Springs?"

"Yeah, that I remember," I said. "It was back a couple a months ago. You brought Saul Goshen to our meeting at the Mexicali Mesa Roadhouse. He was surprised to see me keeping an eye on Frank Sinatra and Paul Anka while I was there, but we had a beer, and I gave him the message I had for him from Bruno Giovanni. You waited for him in the car. After our meeting you left together about eight o'clock. I stayed and took Mr. Sinatra home for the night a little later. I never saw either of you again after that."

"Yeah, that's right. That's what happened." His thick forehead wrinkled as collected his thoughts. "Yeah. Then the next day I got up to drive Mr. Gohlen back to Vegas, but he never showed up. Just disappeared. Nobody's seen him since."

I nodded. "Very strange. I wonder what happened to him."

Donnie couldn't resist a sly smile. "I guess we'll never know."

Now that we had our stories straight, we got back to looking for work. Actually, Donnie was right, I had promised him more work after the job he did for me in Palm Springs. I was thinking I'd probably never see him again, but since he passed the first test and wasn't running away from more dirty work, maybe we should find something for him.

"I'll talk to Mr. Giovanni," I said. "Put in a good word for you and see what we've got.

Look for me here again tomorrow and I'll see what we can do for you."

"Great. Thanks Patrick." He heaved himself out of the small chair, like the large mammal that he was, and took heavy strides around the noisy slot machines and anxious small-time gamblers, past the quieter blackjack tables and out through the lobby – like he actually had somewhere to go. *Look busy, even if you're not*. Donnie had learned that much already.

Later that evening, I was in the office with Bruno Giovanni reviewing my security report on the day's action.

One angry loser had to be thrown out and handed over to the cops for drunk and disorderly, and a card shark trying to cheat the other players got escorted roughly out the back door and had the warning beat into him that he'd now be blackballed from card games everywhere in Vegas. Nothing unusual, just another day at the Golden Goose. We had a reputation for being tough on bad manners. There was also some suspicion by the locals that the tables were tilted just a little in favor of the house. That's why they referred to us as the Wild Goose Casino. The odds were not great for finding the golden goose here. But it was still a favorite for some of the high rollers who were given the VIP treatment, never ripped off, and were attracted to the small private shows with the same well-known stars who filled the showrooms at Caesars Palace and the other flashy big-name casinos. Frank Sinatra was one of those stars who enjoyed the VIP treatment during his private shows at the Golden Goose, especially the parties afterwards with a few friends in the Presidential Suite. It was a special pleasure for me to meet him and be asked to work as his bodyguard and driver whenever Mr. Giovanni wanted to show him a little extra care and attention.

During my meeting with Mr. Giovanni, I mentioned Donnie Bronson and reminded him that he had done the job for us on Saul Goshen. "I sent you to take them both out, Patrick," he said. "It's never a good idea to leave witnesses."

"I know, sir, but I thought it was better to have him do the dirty work and leave me as the witness so he'll have to shut up about it. I think we can use him again now and not have to worry about him changing sides or talking too much to the wrong people."

He nodded slowly, but didn't look convinced.

Mr. Giovanni is a small, impeccably dressed, dark complexioned, middle-aged man with thoughtful piercing dark eyes that can be quite intimidating. Especially if you know some of his history with the Mafia families back in New York. He had ruthlessly protected their interests and did whatever they needed to retain control of their rackets in the East, so they sent him out to Vegas to look after their casino businesses here.

He said, "You need to be careful not to get too smart for your own good, Patrick.

Someday you'll have to prove you're willing to do the killing yourself. It's necessary sometimes to keep people afraid of you. Managing people is always about fear and greed, you know. Keep them loyal and under your control by their fear of you and keep them motivated by their greed."

"That's what I have in mind for Donnie Bronson," I said.

After the meeting at the Golden Goose with Mr. Giovanni, I left the casino and drove back to my room at the Desert Dunes Motel a mile down the Strip and away from the action. On the way, I found myself reflecting on how fear and greed had affected my own decisions in life. Born an Irish-Catholic in San Diego, I was raised with high moral standards and taught to respect authority – my parents at home, the teachers at school, and the priests at church. I started to lose respect and assert my independence as I became more aware of the abuse of authority – first at church, then at school, and finally at work. Never at home. My parents were good people – hardworking, responsible, law-abiding citizens who should have done better for themselves but were never allowed to get ahead by the people above them. Mom was a housekeeper at a hotel in the Gaslamp Quarter and my dad worked on the docks as a longshoreman under the control of the local union. After high school he got me a job there too.

That's where I finally had enough. The union leaders also used fear and greed to manage the longshoremen. Work was handed out at their discretion and they expected kickbacks to encourage consideration for future jobs. It was a reasonable expectation, but one day my foreman demanded an unreasonable piece of my week's wages, so I refused. He decided to send his goon to persuade me to be more reasonable.

I had to beat the crap out of him to win the argument, but I was never going to get another job on the docks, and I might have to deal with bigger and tougher goons next time. So I decided to get out of town and look for work in L.A. instead of hanging around in San Diego. In L.A., I was introduced to the well-paid jobs for tough guys like me in upscale bars and restaurants. One job, and a few incidents with some wanna-be tough guys that worked out in my favour, led me to some new friends in Las Vegas and the work for Mr. Giovanni at the Golden Goose Casino. So far, so good. I'm moving up in his organisation and learning how to manage the fear and the greed, like he said. My own, especially.

After delivering the message to Bruno from Max Palermo, I now had a job to do that might not be so easy for me to keep away from the dirty work. Up to now, I had managed to stay alive and avoid the two cardinal sins with the Mob – stealing from them and ratting them out. So far, those sins were easier for me to avoid than the deadly sin of murder which kept being asked of me. I'd learned from the bosses, though, that it's better to have somebody else pull the trigger and hold good cards to keep them in line, and not turn on you afterwards. Mr. Giovanni might be right, though – someday I might have to pull the trigger myself. I wasn't in any hurry to have to make that decision.

I was enjoying a good life in Vegas, even better than L.A. Mixing with the rich and famous Hollywood stars and spending generously on girlfriends, but I wasn't yet ready to kill somebody to keep up the pace. I'm still a long way from thirty and someday I'll have enough money to settle down safe and comfortable with a good woman. Start on a family like a regular guy. Just not yet. And I still might have to kill somebody first. It could be any day now.

* * *

The next day I sat down again with Donnie Bronson. He arrived at my booth in the coffee shop and slid in opposite me, looking nervous. He knew I was in control and I reinforced the feeling.

"Last time we talked, Donnie, it took a while to get our stories straight, so let me remind you how important that is."

I paused and waited for him to listen carefully to every word. "On the night Mr. Gohlen disappeared, you may not have noticed, but I picked up the shell casings left on the ground, and the next day on the way back to Vegas I picked up the gun you buried on the side of the road in the desert."

Donnie raised his eyebrows and said, "Uh … OK, good. Thanks. I guess that's better than the cops finding the gun and the shells and tying me to his murder."

"That's right. And just to be sure Mr. Giovanni can trust you to join the organisation and work for us, he's now got the gun and shell casings stored away safely for the cops if he ever needs to prove who really killed Saul Gohlen."

"I see," said Donnie. He slumped back into his seat.

"So now that's all settled, you can start Monday," I said.

"We'll put you on the payroll at the casino at a hundred bucks a week. You'll be on security with me and, as you know, the cash bonuses for extra work are real good. We'll have something for you soon enough. Come see me about two in the afternoon on Monday and we'll go to the back office and get you signed up."

He relaxed a little and reached out to shake my hand. "Thanks, Patrick. That's great." His expression showed he was not so sure he should be thanking me.

I gave him a firm shake. "See you, Monday." I slid out of the booth to stride out through the lobby to the street. I did have somewhere to go.

* * *

In our meeting in his office, Mr. Giovanni had accepted my arrangement for Donnie Bronson and that was done, but we had also talked about the message from Max Palermo and what to do about it. He'd given me a strong reply to deliver; he still seemed to be testing whether I could handle the job against tougher guys. I wasn't looking forward to meeting Bennie Fontaine face-to-face. But at least I hadn't been asked to whack him yet.

We were not the only game in town. There was lots of competition among the casinos in Vegas, all working hard to generate the cash demanded by the Mob families back in New York and Chicago. Max Palermo was one of the gangster casino bosses and he was going to be a problem. So I was on my way to the Fortune Palace Casino.

The Fortune Palace didn't look much different from the Golden Goose and the other second tier casinos in Vegas – tall garish neon signage on the street, light bulbs flashing twenty-four hours a day, grandiose entrance hall with polished marble columns and glossy hardwood railings, fake gold trim and dark velvet drapes covering the walls – all overwhelmed by the persistent din of slot machines and anxious small-timer gamblers pulling levers for the spinning wheels to stop on the payline and screaming when it occasionally did.

I parked in the front lot and went in the main entrance, standing tall and conspicuous for the security cameras. I nonchalantly opened my jacket and reached behind me to scratch my back so they could see I had no shoulder harness and holster with a gun in it. Most of us on security working for the casino owners were careful not to carry loaded weapons unless we intended to use them. It was too easy for the police to arrest anyone carrying and haul them in for questioning or give us a few days in jail to cool off before we got to the assigned target. Carrying a weapon was a pretty clear sign that some action was in play.

I walked up to the first security guard I saw and told him I needed to speak to Benny Fontaine. He went around the back and upstairs to the office. A little later I saw Benny come down. He approached me with a scowl.

"What're you doin' here kid? You're not welcome in this place."

"I got a message to deliver to Mr. Palermo."

"Yeah? What's the message?"

"It's not for you, Benny. I got to deliver it to Mr. Palermo myself. Mr. Giovanni insists he gets it exactly the way he gave it to me."

"You're not takin' another fuckin' step into this place. Gimme the message!"

I stared at him and didn't move. "I can't leave until I hear the reply from Mr. Palermo, so I can bring it back it back to Mr. Giovanni, word for word. I'm sure your boss wants me to get it right." He stared back at me and I added, "We're both just doin' our jobs, Benny."

After a long moment and a disgusted look, he said, "Wait here," and signalled to the other security guard to stand in front of me. He turned away and went back upstairs.

After two or three minutes, he came half-way back down the stairs and signalled us to come over. As we arrived at the stairs, he held his hand up to hold the other guy at the bottom of the stairs, then led me up and along the hall to a big office door with brass lettering on a wooden plaque that read, Max Palermo, President, Fortune Palace Enterprises.

As we arrived at the door, Benny turned and placed his large hand on my chest. "Hold on, asshole," he said, "I'm gonna pat you down, then I'm coming in to keep on eye on you."

He did the pat down and opened the door.

I was greeted by another dark scowl from a mean faced, angry man who looked like an extra-large version of Benny. He sat back in his reclining chair with arms folded over his wide chest behind a huge desk with a mess of newspapers strewn across it.

As I stepped forward in front of the desk, I heard Benny say, "Speak up, kid. You got two minutes."

I nodded once and said, "Mr. Palermo, I have a reply from Mr. Bruno Giovanni to your request for a meeting." Palermo held the mean scowl and waited.

I continued. "He says, 'Go fuck yourself.' There's no peace agreement, we're already at war. And he wants you to know what he learned from Hitler during the war. If you hit us, we'll hit you back three times as hard. If you do it again, we'll hit back ten times as hard. That's the message."

I paused before asking, "Do you have a reply for me to take back?"

Palermo held the scowl for a moment, then it slid into a mean smirk. He looked at Benny. "You think we should kill the messenger and send him back in a body bag?"

I caught Benny's shrug out of the corner of my eye. Palermo looked at me again, unfolded his arms to lean forward and put his meaty paws on the desk.

"You got balls, kid," he said. "You knew you just might get killed here and Bruno doesn't give a shit, but you came anyway." He looked at Benny again. "We should hire this sonofabitch instead of killing him. We could use a good soldier willing to take a bullet for the boss."

He leaned back and dropped his hands in his lap. "Get him outta here. I got no more to say to him. Bruno will hear from me directly."

Benny reached out to pull me towards the door, but I turned and moved in that direction without his help. As I headed back down the hallway ahead of him to the top of the stairs, I noticed the other security guy standing in front of an open door to our left talking to somebody with a dark brown fedora pulled forward over his eyes. He was facing away from us but the big body looked vaguely familiar.

What the hell! It was Donnie Bronson.

* * *

After reporting back to Bruno Giovanni, I needed a break from all these games between the casino warlords, so I arranged with Denise to pick her up after work and go out for dinner to one of our favourite Chinese restaurants, the Ruby Red Dining Room at the Stardust Hotel & Casino. I was already anxious and in the mood for romance and Denise very quickly made it worse. It didn't take much for her to go from plain Jane waitress to gorgeous Vegas showgirl and I was devouring her as much as I was the Chinese food. She was a joy to be with and somehow made me feel good about myself without even boasting about what I did all day. Could this be love? Whatever it was, I wanted more.

We were finishing our green tea and laughing at the ridiculous fortune cookie messages –

You must be generous, the universe will reward you. Don't wait for tomorrow, today is the day.

I leaned across the table and said quietly, "Denise, I want you to come to my place before I take you home to your mom, tonight. I really need to have more of you. It's too early to call it a night."

She patted my hand and gave me a shy smile. "I want more of you too, Patrick. But let's be sure to get me home before midnight. I don't want mom worrying about us and I do have to work tomorrow."

"Denise, someday I'm going to convince you to never go home again. But you can decide whenever you want to go home tonight."

She smiled again, then stood up and winked, "Just give me few minutes to get ready for you."

Oh geez. I was already more than ready. I took a deep breath and watched her gorgeous body wrapped in a sleek blue dress sway between the tables on her way to the washroom. I took another sip of the green tea and let my mind wander into thoughts of a happy future with Denise Callahan. Maybe she's the one. After almost two years of chasing skirts in Vegas, she's the only one who's a *keeper,* as my mom used to say. I wonder what comes next for us.

After a while, I stopped daydreaming and came back to the real world in the dining room. It seemed to be taking her longer than usual in the washroom. I glanced at my wristwatch. Had it been forty-five minutes? She was already beautiful enough. She didn't need to do any more to get me in the mood. I was getting impatient to have her alone at home. Was something wrong? Maybe I should check on her.

There was a tap on my shoulder and I heard, "Excuse me, sir, are you Mr. Patrick

Malloy?"

I turned to the waiter standing beside me. "Yes, what's happening?"

He said, "We have a lady on the phone in front who wants to talk to you."

I got up quickly, bumped the table rattling the dinnerware and followed him to the reception desk where the phone lay waiting for me on the sideboard.

It was Denise's mom, Mrs. Callahan. "Patrick, some guy just called me to say Denise is in trouble. She needs your help right away, out back of the Stardust in the parking lot. Please! Go see what's wrong and call me back."

I handed the phone to the waiter and ran back through the restaurant and out the back door to the parking lot. There standing in the front row of cars was Baldy, waiting for me. He tossed his cigarette and ground it into the tarmac with his shoe.

"We got your sweetheart, so don't do anything stupid, asshole, and she won't get hurt."

He turned around and walked straight back through the rows of parked cars to the Oldsmobile sitting parallel to the chain-link fence across the back of the lot and away from the high bright lights in the corners. As we came up closer to the car, the rear driver-side door opened and Skinny stepped out. He held the door open so I could see Denise huddled in the far corner and Benny in the front with his arm across the back of the seat leering at us with a self-satisfied sneer on his ugly mug.

Denise looked messed up, but not hurt, as far as I could tell. I peered in at her. "You OK, baby?" She nodded quickly.

Skinny spoke up. "The bitch bit my hand, so I hadda slap her, that's all. She'll be fine."

I snarled, "You slimy sonofabitch, I'll kill you if you touch her again."

Baldy chipped in. "Get in before we have to slap you next."

Then Benny added, "We have that reply you and Giovanni wanted, kid. We're gonna take you out in the desert for another little chat. Get in the fuckin' car!"

"Let her out first," I yelled. "I'm not getting in until you let her go."

Bennie gave Baldy a fierce look and a quick nod. I saw him coming. He reached for my arm and I jerked it away, then whirled around and slammed a hard right fist straight into his mouth. I felt his teeth cut into my knuckles and the blood from his mouth spurt out over the back of my hand. He staggered backwards, his right leg stuck out straight. I stepped forward, drove my heel hard onto his knee, and heard the pop of ligaments at the same time I heard his scream as he collapsed in a heap beside the car, moaning and gripping his knee in both hands.

Then Skinny came at me. "You bastard," he shouted, "Now you die!"

He was not a fighter – he came at me with his arms outstretched for a deadly bear hug, I guess. I caught him in the jaw with my aching right hand and he dropped straight to the pavement, lying face down and struggling to stay conscious. I stomped on the back of his head and he stopped struggling. He should never have slapped my girlfriend.

I reached for Denise. "Go! Run for it and get inside."

She stepped out and looked at the two tough guys on the ground. They didn't look threatening any longer. I held my left hand over the painful bleeding knuckles. She gave me a quick hug and a kiss on the cheek and a strange look like she didn't recognize me. She ran quickly through the parking lot to the rear door of the restaurant, held it open and looked back, waiting for me.

Benny had watched it all from the front seat of the Oldsmobile. It had happened in a few seconds. I was thinking it had to be the good luck of the Irish that nobody had showed up with a gun. I stepped forward and leaned in through the rear door. "We said three-for-one, right? You want to be number three, Benny?"

He raised his hands, palms forward. "You made your point, kid. You win this round. Now let me clean up this mess and try to explain it to my boss."

"Fine, I'll find another number three," I said.

I watched him get out of the car and heard him mutter, "Useless bastards."

* * *

The next day I reported the incident to Mr. Giovanni. He glanced once at my bandaged right hand and got progressively more agitated and red-faced as he listened. He looked ready to explode but controlled himself before he spoke. "So you think your old friend, Donnie Bronson, is the double-crosser who led them to you and Denise?"

"I don't know how else they would know about me and Denise, where we were and when. I saw Donnie at work during the day and he knew I was leaving early to take Denise to the Red Ruby. I didn't have a chance to talk to him about why he was at the Fortune Palace, but it looks like he was working for them at the same time as he came to us. Maybe they sent him to spy on us in the first place."

"You've given him too many second chances, Patrick. He has to die."

"I know. He's the third man I was thinking of. I think they'll figure it out."

* * *

So now I'm driving out of Vegas southwest toward Barstow with Donnie beside me in the passenger seat. I told him we had a job to do for Mr. Giovanni that was out in this direction at one of the strip bars and whorehouses on the road a few miles from town. The laws on prostitution were looser away from the city, so most of those joints were set up on the main road to southern California, but they still owed a piece of their earnings to the Mob bosses back in Vegas. It was easy to explain to Donnie that we had a job to do out this way.

He's still trying to look like a mobster with the fedora pulled low on his forehead and wearing a sleek black suit jacket. I knew he had his shoulder holster on and his gun loaded for business, so I told him, "It's a bit too obvious you've got a gun under your jacket if we get stopped on the highway, Donnie. Can you take it off and stuff it in the glove compartment for me?"

"Sure, if you think so," he said.

I watched him take it off and wrap it up neatly and push it into the glove compartment. That's part of his problem, he's just too eager to please everybody. Not thinking ahead and taking care of himself. I'm now armed and he's not.

It's hot and bright out on the highway and I don't want to drive until dark, so I'm looking for a spot to pull in out of sight. After a few more miles there's a dirt road off to the right that runs into a gully down a hill and around a corner behind the dry hillside covered in sagebrush and scraggly juniper. "I gotta take a leak, Donnie. I'm just gonna pull over here and get out of sight around the corner a bit."

"OK," he says.

It's only a couple of hundred yards down the dirt road until we're hidden from the highway with nobody in site for miles in any direction. I pull in beside some low bushes and get out. I walk around to the passenger door and Donnie looks up when I pull out my gun and open his door.

"This is the end for you, Donnie"

He's stunned. "What? What the fuck are you doing, Patrick?"

"Get out. You're a dead man, and you damn well know why."

He starts to get out and then takes a quick look at the glove compartment. I grab his arm, yank him out and club him on the side of the head, knocking him to the ground in front of me.

He shuffles up onto his knees and looks up at me, pleading. "C'mon, Patrick, you know me. I'm your friend. I didn't do anything. What are you talking about?"

There's a trickle of blood from above his ear that runs down his cheek and he wipes his hand over it leaving a dirty red streak down to his chin. He looks pathetic, but I have to do my job.

I point the gun at his face. "You can't work for two guys on opposite sides in a war, Donnie. What the hell were you thinking? It's double-crossing and gets you killed every time."

"But I told you, Patrick. I needed the money and had to find work. I started with Palermo at the Fortune Palace before I finally found you at the Golden Goose. I couldn't just quit on them after you hired me and I didn't have much choice to say no to you, either. I was in a trap and trying to get out. But I didn't do anything against you, Patrick. They had a few questions, I had some answers. That's all."

"You set them up to kidnap my girlfriend, then grab me to kill me out in the desert. So this is my answer, Donnie. That's all. That's the way it works."

I reach for him and pull off his goddamn hat and throw it in the dirt. Then I grab a fist full of his hair and hold my gun tight against his cheek under the eye. He cringes and tries to pull away. I hold the handful of hair tighter and press the gun barrel harder into his face.

He looks up. *He is me.*

A kid from California dreaming of making the big leagues. It was never going to happen in baseball or football, but we found a way. Big money, beautiful babes, good times.

But Donnie dead means the dream is over. For him and for me.

* * *

Back in Vegas I have to report to Giovanni again. My future depends on passing this test. I go up to his office as soon as I get back. "It's done. Donnie Bronson has permanently disappeared. Here's his hat and his gun if you want to deliver the evidence, or you want to keep it with the other stuff you already have."

The gun and holster are still neatly wrapped and I place them on the front corner of his desk and put the hat on top. He looks at them for a moment, then reaches forward to pick up the hat. He looks at the bullet hole in it and then puts it back down. There are no bloodstains on the hat.

He doesn't ask any more questions, but he knows I'm not telling him the whole story. I know there'll be another test and he'll need better evidence next time.

* * *

I can't watch Donnie beg for his life. He says, "Please, please, Patrick, I don't deserve to die!" I press the gun harder into his cheek, hold it there and grip his hair in my fist and take three long breaths. The hot desert air is still, there's no other sound. I can smell the drifting scent of sage and juniper. Donnie isn't moving.

I pull the gun away. "God dammit!"

I fire a bullet into his hat and it jumps away in the dust. I fire two more shots into the dirt beside it. "Those were meant for you."

He slumps forward and holds his face in his hands. I can't watch him cry either.

"Get up for Chrissake, Donnie."

He sits back on his heels, drops his chin on his chest and sobs quietly.

I wait a moment for him to settle himself down.

"We need you to disappear, Donnie. After I'm gone you get your ass up to the highway and flag down the bus to Barstow. It'll be going by in about an hour and a bit. Here's fifty bucks to get you on it and go to L.A. Don't go home to San Diego and don't contact anybody you ever knew. Change your name and get lost in the city. If you don't disappear, we're both dead.

"You hear me!"

He nods, and says quietly, "Yes, yes. Thank you, Patrick. You'll never see me again."

I start to get back in the car and look at him slumped in the dirt below the dry desert hillside.

"You don't ever want to see me again."

* * *

LOOKING
FOR ANSWERS

LOOKING FOR ANSWERS

"You're dead to me if I can't trust you, Patrick."

I was sitting in front of Bruno Giovanni in his office at the Golden Goose Casino and I was not enjoying his stern lecture. I thought I had done what I was told. That wasn't the way he saw it. He'd sent me to be Frank Sinatra's bodyguard for the day and now I was here, two days later, in an uncomfortable chair in his large, darkly furnished, dimly lit office, and he was accusing me of lying to him. I felt like I was back in high school being lectured by the vice-principal holding a thick leather strap that he was about to use on the palm of my hand. This was more serious than that.

Dead to me was not an idle expression coming from Bruno Giovanni. He was known as a tough Mafia enforcer from New York City, who was now the boss of one of the Mob's casinos in Las Vegas. Dead and buried in the desert was easy for him to arrange. I should know, I was one of the guys he called on to make it happen. I didn't want to be on the receiving end of that solution. My only way out was to get back in his good books. Trusting me, like he did before this *little chat,* as the security boss, Ron Brendan, had called it when he told me Mr. Giovanni wanted to see me upstairs. I listened carefully for an opening to escape from the verdict of, "Make him disappear. He can't be trusted and he knows too much."

Mr. Giovani glared at me for a long, worrisome moment, then said, "You're lucky, Kid. Frank Sinatra likes you. He came to see me just to save your ass."

Another long pause, and the stern glare returned. "You lied to me. I asked who was at the meeting with Frank and you told me you didn't know. But you did know. You were there and you know Max Palermo as well as I do."

I was about to explain that Mr. Sinatra had asked me not to say who he was with because he wanted Bruno to hear about it from him, nobody else, but Mr. Giovanni continued. "I know he asked you not to tell me, but you work for me, Kid. It doesn't matter what Frank tells you, or anybody else. You gotta be honest with me, tell me everything you know. Don't ever lie to me again or I'm done with you." His dark menacing eyes bored straight into mine and planted the threat deep in my brain.

"Yes, sir," I said. "I'll never make that mistake again. You asked me to spend the afternoon with Mr. Sinatra and do whatever he needed, so I was doing what he asked me to do. Now I understand. I'll always do what *you* want me to do, nobody else."

"You need to learn how it works around here, Kid. Be more careful what you do. I got plans for you. You're smart and tough enough to get by, but you need to get smarter and tougher. I want you to move on to bigger things." His expression relaxed and my shoulders released the tension I was holding back. I waited to hear what was coming next.

With a grim smile, he said, "I got no son, Patrick, maybe I should adopt you."

That was a surprise. Off the hook and into the family?

I couldn't do better than that, if that's what I really wanted. It was a lot to think about as I went back to work on the floor of the Golden Goose Casino.

* * *

After work later that evening, I was getting grilled by my sweetheart, Denise Callahan, who also had some complaints for me. She sat facing me on the end of the sofa at her mom's house on the edge of town, away from the Strip in Las Vegas. Mom wasn't home. Denise still hadn't digested all that had happened during our planned romantic evening a few days earlier. We'd intended a happy ending at my place after dinner, but our plans were interrupted by Max Palermo's thugs from the Fortune Palace Casino. Palermo competed with the Golden Goose and wanted to pressure me to make trouble for Mr. Giovanni. They wanted to use Denise for leverage.

She peered at me from her end of the sofa. "Who are you, Patrick Malloy? I've never seen you like that before."

"You mean the handsome romantic guy trying to seduce you over dinner at the Red Ruby?"

"No! The hard-ass sonofabitch who kicked the shit out of two gangsters in the parking lot when they tried to kidnap me! They had other plans for you too. What the hell, Patrick! Are you a hitman for the Mob now?"

"No, no, Denise. That's not me. I'm no hitman. I just had to defend myself and rescue you, too. You're right though, they were gonna do us damage, maybe even kill us both."

I hesitated before telling her too much, but she'd been dragged into it and had a right to know more about what was going on. "They work for Max Palermo," I said. "He's the gangster who runs the Fortune Palace."

"Like your gangster boss at the Golden Goose." She grimaced and gave me cold look. No invitation to romance there. I couldn't argue. Denise was a waitress at the Golden Goose dining room and her mom worked there too. They knew Bruno Giovanni was the boss of the whole operation.

"Yeah, sort of the same," I said. "They're sworn enemies and sometimes the war includes murder and kidnapping." She was still concerned about where I fit in.

"So you're just a regular soldier in the war between gangsters? Not a hitman? Not a hired gun?"

"Hell no, Denise. I'm just a regular guy, working security, trying to keep the peace."

"If you want to keep the peace, you should work for the good guys and become a cop. Not work as an enforcer for the gangsters."

"Maybe, but this has been pretty good for me so far. It's good money and I'm good at it, keeping my boss happy." *Most of the time*, I thought. "I'll be moving up soon, I think."

I tried to give her my sweetest apologetic look. "That's good for us both, Denise. If we ever decide to settle down, we'll have enough money to get started right."

"I'm not sure I ever want to settle down with a so-called security guy who's working for the Mob. You can kid yourself it's a regular job, Patrick, but not me."

"I've tried regular jobs and it's never worked out for me," I said.

I could have tried to explain my history of getting beaten down by bad bosses when times were hard. Sometimes, I'd had to resort to rough stuff in the past too. That's how I got good at it. Working for the Mob seemed to me the best way to get ahead. And I hadn't killed anybody yet. Denise thinks I should go back to school and learn to do something else. Work for the good guys and stay safe. But it's hard to know who the good guys are.

* * *

The next day, I had a meeting with Ron Brendan, the head of security at the Golden Goose. He'd been asked by Mr. Giovanni to explain exactly how to follow his rules to survive and get ahead in the organisation. I already knew Mob rules, I thought – be completely trustworthy, never steal from them, and don't ever double-cross them – those were the important rules, as far as I knew.

"I don't think I need any lessons in how to get along," I said to Brendan after we got seated in a booth at the back of the dining room away from the noise of the casino floor. "I been here long enough to know what he wants. It's not the first time I've had a tough boss to work for."

"You still got a lot to learn, Kid," he said. "I got a few tips for you to stay alive and keep in Bruno's good books."

"Wait a second," I said. "Why is it you and Bruno keep calling me Kid? I'm not a kid."

Brendan raised his eyebrows. "How old are you?"

I clenched my jaw at the question. "I'll be twenty in a few months."

"That's it, Kid. You ain't a man yet. And you won't make it to manhood unless you get a few things clear in your head. You gotta make some choices about what kinda man you wanna be. This is not a regular job on the docks like you had before, or bouncing drunks at the local bar either. Working in this organisation will change your life if you manage it right or end your life if you don't.

It's already too late for you to walk away and go back to a regular job. You've done too much and you know too much. You either hang on to what you got and try to survive, or you step up and do what you gotta do. Then Bruno might move you up in the organisation. I can help you do that, if it's what you really want." He looked at me thinking about my choices and waited for a response.

"I ain't standing still," I said. "I want more of what I've got. So what do I have to do next to get ahead?"

Brendan then made it very clear what Bruno Giovanni really expected from his close, reliable confidants in the organisation.

"You gotta kill somebody," he said. "That earns respect more than anything. It proves to everybody you're all in. And they know for sure you're hooked because then you need their protection and you ain't gonna mess that up."

"I'm not a cold-blooded killer. That's not why I'm here."

"You'll have to figure it out," he said. "I'll try to find a way to make it easier for you, but the first one is always the hardest. Then you just accept it's part of the job."

I left that meeting with the same dilemma I'd had from the start. How can I work with these guys without becoming a murderer? A few days later, Brendan introduced me to a situation that just might give me an opportunity to pass the test.

* * *

Bruno Giovanni had his Mob bosses to satisfy too, and back in New York there seemed to be questions about somebody skimming cash at the Golden Goose. Brendan explained they weren't satisfied that Bruno was doing enough to fix it and even starting to wonder if he was part of the problem. They were sending their financial guy, Moe Ravinsky, out to Las Vegas to see for himself. There was a lot of pressure on Giovanni to sort it out and he'd asked Brendan to find out who was skimming and end it before Moe Ravinsky arrived.

"But you know who's skimming, Kid," Brendan said. We were sitting in the quiet isolation of his office, but he glanced around nervously before peering at me intently. "It's Bruno, of course. And he doesn't want them to find that out. We know how that worked out for Bugsy Seigel a few years back, he got whacked for it. It didn't matter he was the biggest boss in Vegas at the time, he was killed and left in plain sight on his girlfriend's sofa so everybody got the message – the bosses back in New York know how to take care of any troublemakers with a permanent solution. Bruno doesn't want the bosses back east to have any doubt in their minds when Ravinsky gets here. We have to find a scapegoat who'll take the fall for him. Somebody Bruno has in a position of trust. Somebody we can get a full confession from and then get rid of him to prove we've got everything under control."

I asked him, "You've already got somebody in mind?"

Brendan gave me a long look before replying. "That's what we gotta work on."

I left that meeting wondering who Ron Brendan and Bruno Giovanni might have in mind and started worrying about my friend Sammy Camino, the Shark. He might be the most likely suspect, or scapegoat if that's what they were looking for. Sammy was a longtime pit boss and met all their requirements – managing a lot of cash from the tables and getting it to the counting room and into the vault before arranging for the distribution of the money to the bosses and the banks.

I liked Sammy. He had helped me get sorted out when I first arrived at the Golden Goose. He had a good attitude and a sense of humour about the kind of work we did. "We're just helping people spend their money and have a good time," he told me. "Making sure they behave and nobody gets hurt. It used to be fun for everybody until the gangsters took over and started to fight over who was getting the biggest slice of the pie. Nobody wants to share."

I didn't want Sammy to be the scapegoat for the Mob bosses at the Golden Goose. I needed to find somebody else who deserved to be sacrificed. Maybe I could settle my own score with the bums at Max Palermo's casino who'd tried to maul me and Denise. If it's time for me to kill somebody, they'd be first on my list. I just needed to arrange somehow for them to be involved in skimming at the Golden Goose.

* * *

I decided it might help to level with Denise on my new mission and Bruno Giovanni's problem, since she was involved with my career plans and she also had a grudge to settle with those bastards who tried to kidnap us. I met her at home the next morning before she went to work. After I told her about my meeting with Ron Brendan and before I got to my plans, I discovered she had some news for me herself.

"There's something you should probably know about Ron Brendan," she said. She paused and looked me straight in the eye. "We should have no secrets between us, right?"

I sat back. "Yeah, right, … no secrets."

She took a long breath before adding in a quiet voice, "He's my father."

"What? I thought your father was killed in Europe during the war. That's why your mother was left alone to raise you."

"That's the story Mom likes to tell. But the real story is a little more complicated."

She explained that her mom had a boyfriend who enlisted to join the army during World War II and he went to fight in Europe. He was there for three years before he got killed. During that time, her mom stopped waiting for him and started seeing Ron Brendan. He got her pregnant. They wanted to get married but their families decided they were both too young and didn't want them to start with an illegitimate baby. Her mom decided to have the baby as Mrs. Callahan, using her ex-boyfriend's family name, and never explained to anyone who the real father was. Denise had known Ron Brendan as a family friend from the time she was born, but she didn't know he was her father until her mom told her the truth when she was sixteen.

"Ron has always been very protective of me and my mom and he helped us both get jobs at the Golden Goose," said Denise. "Mom worked in the dining room first and Ron got me the job there when I finished high school. He's been a really good friend to me and Mom, like a real father, all my life."

"Actually, that might explain why he's trying to take good care of me too," I said. "I think he wants you to be with a guy he knows will take good care of you." I was still working on the romantic angle. Then I had a thought. "Did you ask him to keep an eye on me?"

She smiled. "We kind of agreed you might be worth keeping an eye on."

Before I could respond, I heard her mom come down from the bedrooms upstairs and she walked into the living room where we were sitting. "Hello, Patrick," she said. "How are you doing? Taking good care of Denise, I hope. Keeping us all safe?"

"Yes, ma'am," I said, "doing the best I can."

I was looking at her differently now I knew about her history with Ron Brendan, Denise's father. Mrs. Callahan was an attractive lady, slim like Denise, with less prominent curves and darker hair, not blonde. She had the same look about her eyes, with more worry-lines showing her age, although she was probably not more than twenty years older than me and Denise. My mind started to picture her and Ron Brendan together at our age, but those images quickly switched to visions of me and Denise making babies ourselves. *Oh shit, stop that, get back to the present.*

I asked politely, "Are you off to work, Mrs. Callahan?" She was dressed smartly in a pink satin blouse and a long, grey-flannel pleated skirt, made-up with bright red lipstick and light-blue eye shadow.

"Yes," she said with a smile. "I have to do my bit to help pay for the house and the groceries. The tips are not so good at my age, Denise does much better than I ever did, so I gave up waitressing and have a good job in the office at the Golden Goose now, away from the rambunctious gamblers and bright lights in the casino. The hours are better and the pay's good too."

"Sounds like a good move," I said.

"It was," said Mrs. Callahan. "You should think about an office job or something quieter and safer yourself, Patrick. Are you ready to leave security at the casino yet?"

"Not yet. Besides, it gives me a chance to keep an eye on Denise and make sure she's safe and sound." I smiled. "Like you said."

She looked unconvinced and leaned in to kiss Denise goodbye. "You two behave now, I'll see you later."

After she had gone and the door was closed behind her, I said, "She worries too much."

Denise replied, "You don't worry enough."

Maybe she was right, I had a lot to worry about if I was going to stay alive and move onward and upward with the gangsters at the Golden Goose. Ron Brendan had made it sound easy. All I had to do was find a scapegoat for Bruno Giovanni skimming cash from the casino, get a confession out of him, then kill him. That makes Bruno happy and I'm his new hero. Maybe not his new favorite son, but at least I'd be less likely to get whacked myself.

I decided the next thing I needed to do was speak to Sammy Camino. I didn't want him to get whacked either, and he might have some better ideas on how to solve Bruno Giovanni's problem.

* * *

Later that evening during his break, I asked Sammy to come over to a quiet corner in the hotel lobby beside the casino entrance and have a coffee with me. One of the hostesses came over and set two coffees on cocktail napkins on the low glass table in front of us.

She looked up to smile at me and ask, "Anything else?"

We shook our heads. "No thanks," I said.

Sammy took a long sip of the steaming hot coffee and sat back. "So what's up, Patrick?"

I took a moment for my own coffee, dumping in a packet of sugar and stirring it once before taking a taste and putting it down again. "I need the advice of the Shark, Sammy," I said. "You told me once that before you became a dealer at the casinos, they called you the Shark because you were the killer they put into dangerous waters when the Mob needed a problem solved." I waited for him to interrupt and correct that version of his history, but he sat still and let me continue.

"Now I have a problem to solve and it may be a problem for you too," I said. "The people working on it just might decide that killing you is a solution for them. I want to avoid that happening."

He frowned. "What the hell are you talking about, Kid?"

I told him about Moe Ravinsky coming from New York because of the suspicions of skimming at the Golden Goose and Ron Brendan's plan to have a scapegoat delivered dead to avoid any suspicion that Giovanni was behind the missing cash that should be going to New York.

"I think you might be a likely scapegoat," I said. "You're in charge of the tables, you supervise the counting and delivery of cash to the vault. You're a likely suspect if anyone's skimming."

He nodded and took a long thoughtful sip of coffee before responding. "We all have a problem if anybody's caught skimming cash at the Golden Goose," he said. "There'll be hell to pay. And Ron Brendan is a suspect as much as me. He's responsible for casino security and he also supervises all the cash coming off the floor into the vaults."

He was right. I had thought the same thing.

I asked, "How well do you know Ron Brendan?"

He shrugged. "We go way back. Together at school — cheating on exams, smashing bodies at football, swapping girlfriends, drinking beer, driving hot rods. Good times." He smiled at the memories. "Then we ended up working together at the casinos. Those were always the best jobs after high school."

"You shared girlfriends?" That led me to another question. "Did you know Denise's mom, Mrs. Callahan, back then too?"

"Louise Henderson was her name then. Oh, yeah. She was a sweetheart, but never my girlfriend. Too shy and quiet for me." He smiled to himself again at the memories of his high school days in Las Vegas.

"How about Ron Brendan?"

"That's a longer story, but he was never her boyfriend in high school. They hooked up later, but it didn't work out then either." He paused and I wondered how much of the story he really knew.

"Anyway," he said, "let's get back to our problem and try to work that out." I agreed.

Suddenly we were interrupted by a loud commotion at the front entrance to the casino. We heard terrified shrieking and screaming and a crowd rushed in the front door from outside. I heard the squeal of tires burning rubber and a car roaring away.

Somebody yelled, "Call the police! They threw a body out of that car!"

"What the hell's going on," I said to Sammy.

We rushed out to the driveway in front, broke through a small crowd of shocked spectators, and saw the uniformed doorman and parking valet staring at the body of a man in a grey suit sprawled on the pavement. A sack over his head had fallen away to reveal a deep gash across his throat with blood leaking down his neck and onto his shirt collar.

"Okay, everybody stand back," I hollered. "The police are on the way. Go inside and stay there. If you saw anything, they'll want to talk to you." The crowd backed away and most stood watching; nobody went inside.

I turned to the doorman, "Give me your coat," I said. Then to the valet and bell boys standing by, "Cordon off the entrance and direct guests through the side entrance." I took the doorman's coat and threw it over the body to cover the ugly sight without disturbing anything. Sammy pulled it straight to cover the other side and came back to stand beside me.

"You know who that is?" he asked. I shook my head, thinking maybe I'd seen him around, maybe a regular at the casino. Sammy stepped closer and whispered. "It's Larry Santorini. He was our guy undercover at the Fortune Palace. I think this is Max Palermo's way of telling us he knows what he was up to and where he came from."

After the police had come and gone and the body had been removed, I caught up with Sammy again and had more questions for him. We sat behind his station at the blackjack tables. We spoke quietly, leaning forward with our heads close together.

"How do you know he was our guy at the Fortune Palace?" I asked.

"He used to work security here, then just disappeared for a while. The rumour was that he got fired for cheating at cards or something. A few months later he showed up at the Fortune Palace. Max Palermo probably thought he was hiring him to learn about Bruno's operations, but he was more likely sent by Bruno to get inside Max's operation."

"What the hell is the point of that? They already know everything there is to know about each other's operations."

"Well, they'll never know enough and the spying will never stop. It's useful to have a trusted insider screwing with the competition if he can. Mess up their business and make them look bad. Both sides love to do that."

I thought about it for a moment. "You mean like having an insider set up a skimming operation and arrange for the boss to get blamed for it."

Sammy gave me a shark's smile. "You catch on fast, Kid."

I was beginning to think we had an insider at the Golden Goose doing exactly that. But I wasn't sure how to find out more without placing suspicion on Sammy or Ron Brendan. I would soon learn that Ron Brendan was not waiting for me to pin the skimming on him or anybody else. He had his own plan.

While he was working on his plan, though, I was working on mine. Denise was part of it and she liked the idea of going after Max Palermo's thugs and making them the scapegoats so we could get our revenge on them at the same time as solving Bruno Giovanni's problem. But first we had to be sure Ron Brendan didn't get caught in the crossfire.

The next evening after Denise finished her shift in the dining room, we had arranged a meeting with Brendan. We joined him at his regular small table in a corner at the back of the bar. After explaining we wanted to talk to him together because we thought he might be in trouble because of us, Denise was quick to interject, "Patrick knows you're my dad, Ron. And he knows you're very protective of me and Mom and you take a special interest in him because he's important to me."

Ron looked a little concerned that I might know too much too soon, then he nodded and smiled. "The Kid's not good enough for you yet, sweetheart, but I'm working on him."

I said, "I appreciate you trying to help me out here, Ron, but we're actually worried about you. That's what we wanted to talk about."

Ron shook his head. "You don't need to worry about me. I been able to take care of myself for a long time now."

"We know that," I said, "but we think maybe your interest in protecting Denise and her mom makes you vulnerable to threats from a guy like Max Palermo. Like his gang did to me. They grabbed Denise and held her hostage to draw me into a trap."

"I can handle Max Palermo and his bums. They don't scare me and you shouldn't worry about it. I'm sure Max doesn't know about my connection to Denise and her mom."

I looked skeptical. "It's not a big secret among the old timers who knew you back in high school, Ron. Some of them work here and some of them work for Max Palermo too."

He glanced at Denise before giving me a hard stare. "You been talking to Sammy," he said.

I nodded and thought hard about getting to what we really wanted to talk about. "It's more important what I learned from Sammy about Larry Santorini," I said. "He was murdered by Palermo and thrown out at our front door yesterday because he was working for Bruno at the Fortune Palace." Ron frowned and waited for me to continue. "He was planted there as an insider to make trouble for Palermo," I said. "I'm sure Palermo is trying to do the same here. It would make sense for him to pressure somebody on the inside here rto skim cash and set up Bruno to get blamed for it."

I let that idea settle for moment. Then I asked him, "Are you that guy, Ron?"

Ron's frown turned to a fierce glare. "You're way out of line, Kid. That's nuts. I don't appreciate you even talking about it in front of Denise. You really do have a lot to learn." He got up from his chair. "I'll see you later."

As he walked away, I turned to look at Denise. She looked more concerned than when we had arrived.

* * *

It was a couple of days later that Ron Brendan called me to meet him in his office. As soon as I got there, he said, "I'm still pissed-off at you for suggesting I was involved in skimming cash to screw Bruno, Patrick, so I want to get this sorted out, once and for all."

He explained he wanted me to meet him and Sammy the Shark later that evening in the counting room and he would tell us both how this was going to end. I knew the counting room – a secure concrete-walled room in the basement, bullet-proof and bomb proof, in front of the main vault – used several times a day to receive cash from the smaller vaults behind the cashiers in the casino for counting and transfer into the main vault. I'd been assigned many times to guard transport of the cash drawers on rolling carts into the back service elevators and down to the counting room. The room had a solid steel door at the entrance with the main vault filling the wall at the other end. The white concrete sidewalls were lined with shelves and filing cabinets and a desk was set in the back corner facing the long broad table that was surrounded by black folding chairs in the middle of the room.

We met there at eleven that evening.

* * *

The three of us are sitting at the long table. Ron is at the end with me and Sammy facing each other on either side of him. Ron and Sammy were already there when I arrived.

Ron asks if I brought my gun. I nod, it's in the shoulder holster under my suit jacket. "Put it on the table," he says. He reaches for his own and puts it there. Sammy does the same, then we both look at him waiting to hear what's next.

Ron reaches down to lift up the large black leather briefcase I hadn't noticed sitting on the floor beside his chair. He thumps it on the table between the three guns and they bounce where they lie. Ron lays the briefcase flat, pops the locks, and opens it to reveal the bundles of cash inside. I'm trying to calculate how much in tens of thousands, maybe hundreds of thousands, when he drops the lid and snaps the locks shut again.

He sits back and says, "OK, now we have the evidence in front of us and we're all here – the crook, the witness, and the executioner. We just have to decide who's who. Who's going to die today."

He takes a deep breath, looks first at Sammy for long moment, then he turns to me.

"So do we put it on Sammy?" he says. "If it's not him, it must be me."

He places his hands on the table and leans toward me. "Or is it you, Kid?"

Sammy's shaking his head. He reaches for his gun, pulling back his suit jacket to put it in the holster on his belt. "I'm leaving," he says. "You two are on your own."

"Nobody's leaving until we're done here," says Ron. He picks up his gun and points it at Sammy, who sits back and holds his hands in his lap.

Ron turns his gun on me. "So it's you or me, Patrick," he says. "One of us has to die. Then it's over. That's how this has to end."

He can't be right. It makes no sense. My mind is racing for better answers. I'm staring at the gun aimed at my head. I look at the knuckles of Ron's fist wrapped around the handle and see his finger start to squeeze the trigger.

I'm not going to sit here and watch the bullet leave the barrel!

I grab my gun off the table and dive to the floor, roll on my back and slide up to brace my back against the wall. I raise my gun and point it at Ron standing at the end of the table. Sammy backs away toward the far wall, gun in hand.

I yell, "Don't do it, Ron!"

I'm looking directly into his gun barrel and see it shift slightly to the left as the muzzle flashes and I feel the bullet swish past my ear over my shoulder and hit the wall behind me before I hear the shot.

I can't shoot back at him. *He's Denise's father!*

He shoots again and another bullet smacks into the wall over my other shoulder. I hold my gun firmly in two hands pointed at Ron's chest, but my finger stays off the trigger. I still can't do it. It's so quiet. The sound of gunshots fades into the silence scented by the smell of hot gunpowder. I can hear my own breathing and nothing else.

Ron's gun is pointing at me again and aimed at my forehead. His aim is steady and his finger is firmly on the trigger.

Suddenly, the silence is shattered by loud shots and I see the splatter of blood in two spots on Ron's chest.

He stiffens and drops his gun to the floor. Then he falls backward, bumps against the wall and slides awkwardly to the floor beside the door. He flops onto his back, eyes wide, looking at the ceiling. He coughs faintly. He lies flat with his legs stretched out and raises one hand to hold against the wounds in his chest. The blood trickles out between his fingers.

Sammy lowers his smoking gun and stands still, watching him die. I go to Ron and kneel beside him on the floor, lean in and put my hand on his shoulder.

Ron speaks weakly, "This is good, Kid. We've solved Bruno's problem." He coughs and tries to catch his breath. "Now you're the hero Bruno wants you to be." He wheezes. "You'll even get the girl in the end."

I squeeze his shoulder and look at the blood soaking into his shirt.

He looks at me and moans, "Next time you gotta be the Shark." His hand slips off his chest. He groans, "Be the Shark." He squeezes his eyes shut, and stiffens once before his body releases it's hold on life and flattens against the floor. He's dead.

I look at Sammy who's wiping the prints off his gun with a handkerchief. He holds it out to me by the barrel. "Give me your gun," he says. "Get your fingerprints on this one. You can claim you killed him in self defense, I can't."

Before the police arrive, we agree on our story. Ron has to be the scapegoat. He died trying to escape after we confronted him with the briefcase full of cash and demanded the truth. He confessed he was working for Max Palermo. We're never going to tell anyone that he was doing it to protect Denise and her mom from threats by Palermo. The only way out was for Ron to die.

I still have more questions than answers. I look at Sammy. "Did he ask you to kill him?"

"No," he says. He shakes his head slowly. "He was trying to let you decide if you could do it. But you should know he would have killed you if you couldn't. That would also have ended it for him and solved his problem with Bruno."

* * *

The hard part for me was not explaining it all to Bruno Giovanni, it was explaining it to Denise. Again she surprised me.

"After we spoke to Ron, I talked to Mom about it," she said. "Mom told me she also had some concern that Ron was under suspicion for being involved in the skimming operation at the Golden Goose. Working late in the office with the accountants, she'd heard the gossip and tried to warn Ron to stay away from getting caught stealing from Mr. Giovanni. He wouldn't listen to her either. Told her not to worry about him."

I didn't say anything about my suspicions that her mom, and Sammy too, knew more than they were telling us. They were probably both helping Ron in the skimming operation, he couldn't do it alone and cover it up. And maybe Giovanni was behind it all along.

I told her I thought Ron had decided the only way out was for him to die, and that I should be the one to do it and advance my reputation as a tough guy for Bruno Giovanni. I admitted to her I couldn't do it, but Sammy the Shark did.

She gave me a sad smile. "I'm glad to know you're not that tough a tough guy."

"I think it was Ron's way of passing the torch," I said. "He knew his days were numbered at the Golden Goose." I gave her a hug and a kiss on the cheek and after a quiet moment, I added, "Now I'm the one responsible for protecting you and your mom."

I stepped back. "And I have more work to do for Mr. Giovanni, too." She raised her eyebrows into a question mark.

I told her, "He wants me to do the hit on Max Palermo."

"Do it," she said. "We owe Ron that much."

* * *

AUTHOR - DELVIN CHATTERSON

Delvin Chatterson is the internationally acclaimed author of the Dale Hunter Thriller Series which started with NO EASY MONEY published in 2018, introducing entrepreneur Dale Hunter and his crime-fighting buddy, Frank the Fixer, in an explosive mix of crime and corruption in the international computer business of the 1980s. The series of standalone novels continues with SIMPLY THE BEST and MERGER MANIAC published in 2019, BAD BOYS IN BOSTON and CRASH LANDING in 2024, and WHATEVER IT TAKES coming in 2025. Del is also working on more novels and writing short stories, including The Kid from California - Short Stories - Volumes 2 and 3.

As a former entrepreneur, business advisor, and cheerleader for enlightened entrepreneurship, Del has written extensively on business topics for decades and continues to write on entrepreneurship under the pen name of *Your Uncle Ralph* at LearningEntrepreneurship.com.

Originally from the Rocky Mountains of British Columbia, Del has lived and worked for most of the last fifty years in the fascinating French-Canadian city of Montreal.

Author Website: **DelvinChatterson.com**

Connect with Del on: **Facebook** - **Twitter** - **Instagram** - **YouTube**

THE DALE HUNTER THRILLER SERIES

NO EASY MONEY - *You never win playing by the rules...* First in the series of Dale Hunter Crime Novels, an explosive mix of crime, cash and computers in the 1980s. Entrepreneurs face challenges every day. It's hard to be a hero. Dale Hunter is facing threats from the Montreal Mafia and dirty dealing by crooked business associates. He wants to survive and not play by gangster rules. It will require courage and creativity and the support of some new friends. Somebody is going to get killed.

SIMPLY THE BEST - *It may be simple, it's never easy* Dale Hunter is again up against the gangsters who tried to murder him once and are now threatening his family. Meanwhile, Hunter's new partner in Taiwan is dragging him into smuggling schemes with the Triads. The danger escalates. Hunter's escape may be simple, but it's never easy.

MERGER MANIAC - *Some offers have to be refused* Dale Hunter is trying to save his business from competitive threats in the rapidly evolving computer business of the 1980s. He's looking for partners when he's suddenly approached by the Mafia to participate in their money laundering schemes. Hunter has to walk a dangerous tightrope to avoid getting dragged into more crime and corruption.

BAD BOYS IN BOSTON - *It's just business, never personal* Thirty years after fighting crime and corruption in the 1980s, Dale Hunter and Frank the Fixer are now drawn into rescuing a niece kidnapped into sex trafficking and online pornography by Russian gangsters in Boston. Dale and Frank follow a treacherous trail into the dangerous and violent international sex trade that also exposes Frank's tragic family history in Africa and more violent threats closer to home in Montreal.

CRASH LANDING - *Public pressure, private pain* Dale Hunter is fighting to save his business from disaster, when his business associate is found dead in an apparent suicide. The police immediately report it as a suspicious death, possibly murder. They pursue a widening web of likely suspects, including Dale Hunter. Then connections to organised crime are revealed and it suddenly gets more complicated and more dangerous. The only way out is to find the truth before Hunter becomes the next victim.

WHATEVER IT TAKES – *Trust nobody* Dale Hunter is shocked to discover that his friend and longtime mentor and role model as a successful entrepreneur, is a completely ruthless, greedy and ambitious egotist, probably crooked, and possibly a murderer. Hunter is asked to help extricate his friend from the dirty deals with criminals manipulating local politicians for profit in major municipal projects and instead of running for cover, Hunter gets drawn into the lethal conspiracies himself.

HIGH PRAISE FOR THE DALE HUNTER SERIES

"Chatterson's language conveys mayhem with a brevity that practically demands attention. Action sequences are rapid fire and corrosive … offset by threatening undertones. Chatterson pens crime drama that is fast-paced and involved."

— INDIE READER REVIEW

"Great read! … I had to get up in the middle of the night to finish it!"

— Ken Collins (Canada)

"I read this book in one day … How do I get my hands on his next book?"

— Margaret Heaton (USA)

Amazing! An absolutely outstanding writer! Hooked and thoroughly entertained. …. a captivating author."

— Peter J. Malouf (Canada)

"I liked it a lot! And I was there, in the computer business of the 1980s. I'm telling all my friends, very impressive!"

— Gilles Gaudet (Canada)

"Welcome to the '80s Business World. I love how the story flowed and the intensity continued to increase, keeping you reading to the very end. Keeps you on the edge of your seat for an intense and exciting read. Enjoy the ride! It's a fast one!"

— Amanda Leeber (USA), Amazon.com Review

"Loved it right from the beginning! The passion between the characters had me not wanting to put it down. A definite must read! Looking forward to reading book two."

— Jasmin Moore, Goodreads Reviewer

MORE SHORT STORIES
FROM DELVIN CHATTERSON

PUBLISHED IN MYSTERY & SUSPENSE MAGAZINE:

FALL 2023: *FAMILY FIRST – FALL2023.PDF*

FEATURE ARTICLES & REVIEWS- CHATTERSON

SEE ALSO: WWW.DELVINCHATTERSON.COM/SHORT-STORIES

UNDERGROUND RAGE

A LONG WALK

THE HISTORY OF COMPUTERS AS I KNOW IT

A LONG PADDLE INTO THE WIND